Rikki~Tikki~Tavi

Rikki~Tikki~Tavi

BY **RUDYARD KIPLING**

ADAPTED AND ILLUSTRATED BY **JERRY PINKNEY**

Morrow Junior Books • *New York*

Pencil, Prismacolor, and watercolor on Arches watercolor paper were used for the full-color illustrations.
The text type is 14-point New Baskerville.

Copyright © 1997 by Jerry Pinkney

Printed in Hong Kong by South China Printing Company (1988) Ltd.

1 3 5 7 9 10 8 6 4 2

Library of Congress Cataloging-in-Publication Data
Pinkney, Jerry.
Rikki-tikki-tavi/by Rudyard Kipling; adapted and illustrated by Jerry Pinkney.
p. cm.
Summary: A courageous mongoose thwarts the evil plans
of Nag and Nagaina, two big cobras who live in the garden.
ISBN 0-688-14320-2 (trade)—ISBN 0-688-14321-0 (library)
[1. Mongooses—Fiction.   2. Cobras—Fiction.   3. India—Fiction.]
I. Kipling, Rudyard, 1865–1936. Rikki-tikki-tavi.   II. Title.
PZ7.P633475Ri 1997   [Fic]—DC21   96-51194   CIP AC

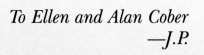

To Ellen and Alan Cober
—J.P.

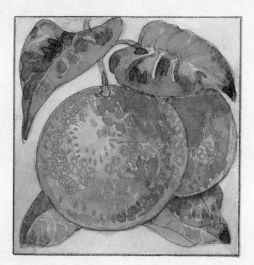

This is the story of the great war that Rikki-tikki-tavi fought, all by himself, through the English family's house in India.

Rikki-tikki-tavi was a mongoose, with fur and a tail like a cat's and a head like a weasel's. One day a summer flood washed him out of the burrow where he lived with his father and mother and floated him, kicking and clucking, down a roadside ditch. He found a stick floating near him, and he held on to it until he fainted. When he revived, he was lying in the middle of a garden path, very wet indeed, and a little boy was saying, "Here's a dead mongoose. Let's have a funeral."

"No," said his mother. "Let's take him in and dry him. Perhaps he isn't really dead."

They took him into the house, where a big man picked him up and said he wasn't dead, just tired. So they wrapped him in cotton and warmed him over a little fire, and he opened his eyes and sneezed.

"Now," said the big man, who was the boy's father, "don't frighten him, and we'll see what he'll do."

It is the hardest thing in the world to frighten a mongoose, because he is full of curiosity from nose to tail. The motto of the mongoose family is "Go and find out," and Rikki-tikki was a true mongoose. He looked at the cotton, decided it wasn't good to eat, ran all around the table, sat up, scratched himself, and jumped on the boy's shoulder.

"Don't be frightened, Teddy," said his father. "That's his way of making friends."

"He tickles!" said Teddy. Rikki-tikki snuffled at the boy's ear and climbed down to the floor, where he sat rubbing his nose.

"Is he so tame because we helped him?" asked Teddy's mother.

"All mongooses are like that," said the husband. "If Teddy doesn't pick him up by the tail, he'll run in and out of the house all day long. Let's give him something to eat."

They gave him a little piece of raw meat, which Rikki-tikki liked immensely. "There are more things to find out about in this house," he said to himself, "than all my family could find out in all their lives. I shall certainly stay and find out." He spent the day roaming around the house. He nearly drowned in the bathtub, put his nose in the ink on a desk, and burned it on the end of the big man's cigar. When Teddy went to bed, Rikki-tikki climbed up too.

Teddy's mother and father came in before they went to bed, and Rikki-tikki was awake on the pillow. "I don't like this," said Teddy's mother. "He might bite."

"He won't," said the father. "Teddy's safer with that little animal than with a watchdog. If a snake came into his room—" But Teddy's mother wouldn't think of anything so awful.

Early in the morning Rikki-tikki came to breakfast on the porch riding on Teddy's shoulder, and they gave him banana and some boiled egg, and he sat on all their laps one after the other.

Then Rikki-tikki went out into the backyard to see what was to be seen. It was a large yard with rosebushes as big as houses, lime and orange trees, and clumps of bamboos. Rikki-tikki scuttled up and down the garden, snuffling here and there, until he heard very sad voices in a thornbush. It was Darzee, the tailorbird, and his wife. They had made a beautiful nest by pulling two big leaves together and stitching up the edges, and had filled the inside with fluff.

"What's the matter?" asked Rikki-tikki.

"We are miserable," said Darzee. "One of our babies fell out of the nest yesterday, and Nag ate him."

"Hmm!" said Rikki-tikki. "That is very sad, but I am a stranger here. Who is Nag?"

Darzee and his wife cowered down in the nest without answering, for from the thick grass at the foot of the bush there came a low hiss—a horrid cold sound. Then inch by inch out of the grass rose up the head of Nag, the big cobra, and he was five feet long from tongue to tail. When he had lifted one-third of himself clear of the ground, he swayed like a dandelion tuft in the wind, and he looked at Rikki-tikki with the wicked snake's eyes that never change their expression, whatever the snake may be thinking.

"Who is Nag?" said he. "*I* am Nag. Look, and be afraid!"

Rikki-tikki was afraid for a minute, but it is impossible for a mongoose to stay frightened for very long. Rikki-tikki had never met a live cobra before, but his mother had fed him on dead ones, and he knew that a mongoose's job is to fight and eat snakes. Nag knew that too, and at the bottom of his cold heart he was afraid.

"Well," said Rikki-tikki, "I'm looking, but do you think it is right for you to eat baby birds?"

Nag was watching for movement in the grass behind Rikki-tikki. He knew that mongooses in the garden meant death sooner or later for him and his family. He dropped his head a little and said, "Let's talk. You eat eggs, why shouldn't I eat birds?"

"Behind you! Look behind you!" said Darzee.

Rikki-tikki jumped up in the air as high as he could go, and just under him whizzed by the head of Nagaina, Nag's wicked wife. She had crept up behind him as he was talking, to kill him, and he heard her hiss as the stroke missed. He came down almost across her back and bit, but he did not bite long enough, and he jumped away from the whisking tail, leaving Nagaina torn and angry.

"Wicked, wicked Darzee!" said Nag, lashing up as high as he could reach toward the nest, but Darzee had built it out of reach of snakes.

Rikki-tikki felt his eyes getting hot and angry, and he sat back on his tail and hind legs like a little kangaroo and chattered with rage. But Nag and Nagaina had disappeared in the grass. Rikki-tikki did not follow them, for he did not feel sure he could manage two snakes at once. So he trotted off to the gravel path near the house and sat down.

Rikki-tikki was just a young mongoose, and he was very pleased that he had managed to escape an attack from behind. When Teddy came running down the path, Rikki-tikki was ready to be petted.

But just as Teddy was leaning down, something squirmed in the dust, and a tiny voice said, "Be careful. I am death!" It was Karait, the little brown snakeling that lies on the dusty ground in India and whose bite is as dangerous as the cobra's.

Rikki-tikki's eyes grew angry again, and he danced up to Karait with the strange rocking, swaying motion that he had inherited from his family. It looks very funny, but it is so perfectly balanced that he could fly off in any direction he wanted, and in dealing with snakes this is an advantage. He rocked back and forth, looking for a good place to hold. Karait struck. Rikki jumped sideways, and the wicked little dusty head lashed right near his shoulder.

Teddy shouted to the house, "Come look! Our mongoose is killing a snake." And Rikki-tikki heard a scream from Teddy's mother. His father ran out with a stick, but by the time he came up, Rikki-tikki had sprung, jumped on the snake's back, bitten as high up as he could, and rolled away. That bite paralyzed Karait, and Rikki-tikki was just going to eat him up from the tail to the head, after the custom of his family, when he remembered that a big meal makes a slow mongoose.

He went away for a dust bath under the bushes, while Teddy's father beat the dead snake. "What's the use of that?" thought Rikki-tikki. "I've already settled it all." Then Teddy's mother picked him up and hugged him, saying that he had saved Teddy's life. Rikki-tikki did not understand the fuss. Teddy's mother might just as well have hugged Teddy for playing in the mud. Rikki was thoroughly enjoying himself.

That night at dinner, walking among the glasses on the table, he could have stuffed himself with good things but did not. Though it was very pleasant to be petted, he remembered Nag and Nagaina, and from time to time he would give his war cry of *"Rikk-tikk-tikki-tikki-tchk!"*

Teddy carried him to bed and insisted that Rikki-tikki sleep under his chin. But as soon as Teddy was asleep, he went for his nightly walk around the house, and in the dark he ran up against Chuchundra, the muskrat, creeping near the wall. Chuchundra is a scared little beast. He whimpers and cheeps all night, trying to make up his mind to run into the middle of the room, but he never gets there.

"Don't kill me," said Chuchundra. "Rikki-tikki, don't kill me."

"Do you think a snake killer kills muskrats?" asked Rikki-tikki scornfully.

"Those who kill snakes get killed by snakes," said Chuchundra. "And how am I to be sure Nag won't mistake me for you some dark night?"

"There's no danger," said Rikki-tikki. "Nag is in the garden, and you don't go there."

"My cousin, the rat, told me—," said Chuchundra, and then he stopped.

"Told you what?"

"Hush! Nag is everywhere, Rikki-tikki. Can't you *hear*?"

Rikki-tikki listened. The house was as still as still, but he could just catch a soft *scratch-scratch* sound—a noise as quiet as the footsteps of a fly on a windowpane—the dry scratch of a snake's scales on brick.

"That's Nag or Nagaina," he said, "and whoever it is, is crawling into the bathroom drain. Thank you, Chuchundra."

He crept to Teddy's bathroom, but there was nothing there, and then to Teddy's parents' bathroom. At the bottom of the plaster wall there was a brick pulled out to make a drain for the bathwater, and as Rikki-tikki listened, he heard Nag and Nagaina whispering together in the moonlight.

"When the house is emptied of people," said Nagaina, "*he* will go away, and then the garden will be ours again. Go in quietly, and remember that the big man who killed Karait is the first one to bite. Then come out, and we will hunt for Rikki-tikki."

"But are you sure we must kill the people?" asked Nag.

"Yes. When there were no people in the house, did we have a mongoose in the garden? As long as the house is empty, we are king and queen of the garden. Remember that as soon as our eggs hatch, our children will need room and quiet."

"I had not thought of that," said Nag. "I will go, but there's no need to hunt for Rikki-tikki. I will kill the man and woman, and the child if I can. Then the house will be empty, and Rikki-tikki will leave."

Rikki-tikki tingled all over with rage at this, and then Nag's head came through the drain, and his five feet of cold body followed it. Angry as he was, Rikki-tikki was very frightened when he saw the size of the cobra. Nag raised his head and looked into the bathroom, and Rikki could see his eyes glitter in the dark.

"When Karait was killed, the man had a stick," said the snake, "but when he comes to bathe in the morning, he won't have it. I'll wait here till he comes. Nagaina—do you hear me?—I'll wait here till daytime."

There was no answer, so Rikki-tikki knew Nagaina had gone away. Nag coiled himself down, coil by coil, around the bottom of the water jar that was used to fill the bath. Rikki-tikki stayed as still as death. After an hour he began to move, muscle by muscle, toward the jar. Nag was asleep, and Rikki-tikki looked at him, wondering how to attack. "If I don't break his back at the first jump," thought Rikki, "he can still fight. And if he fights— Oh, Rikki!

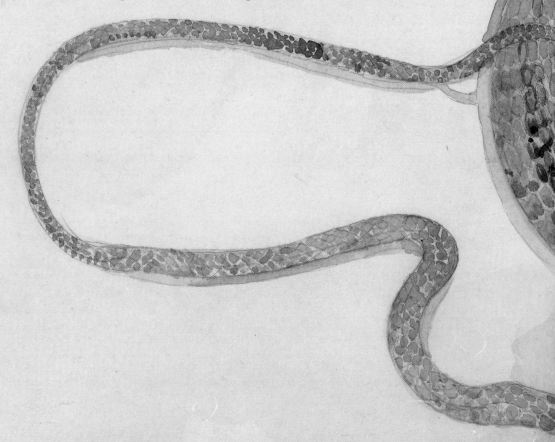

"It must be the head," he decided finally. "And I must not let go."

Then he jumped. As he bit, Rikki braced his back against the water jar to hold down the snake's head. Then he was battered back and forth as a toy is shaken by a dog—back and forth, up and down, and around in circles—but he held on as the snake's body whipped across the floor and banged against the side of the bathtub. He closed his jaws tighter and tighter, for he was sure he would be banged to death, and, for the honor of his family, he wanted to be found with his teeth locked. He was dizzy, aching, and felt shaken to pieces when something went off like a thunderclap just behind him, and red fire singed his fur. Teddy's father had been wakened by the noise and had fired a shotgun into Nag.

Rikki-tikki held on with his eyes shut, for now he was sure he was dead, but the man picked him up and said, "It's the mongoose again. The little guy has saved *our* lives now."

When morning came, Rikki-tikki was very stiff but well pleased with himself. "Now I have Nagaina to deal with, and she will be worse than five Nags. And there's no knowing when the eggs will hatch. I must go see Darzee," he said.

Without waiting for breakfast, Rikki-tikki ran to the thornbush where Darzee was singing a song of triumph at the top of his voice. The news of Nag's death was all over the garden, because his body had been put on the garbage heap.

"Oh, you stupid tuft of feathers!" said Rikki-tikki. "Is this the time to sing?"

"Nag is dead, dead, dead!" sang Darzee. "The valiant Rikki-tikki caught him by the head and held tight. The big man brought the bang stick, and Nag broke in two pieces! He will never eat my babies again."

"You're safe enough in your nest there," said Rikki-tikki, "but it's war for me down here. Stop singing a minute, Darzee."

"For the great Rikki-tikki's sake, I will stop," said Darzee. "What is it, O killer of the terrible Nag?"

"Where is Nagaina?"

"On the garbage heap by the stables, mourning for Nag, great Rikki-tikki of the white teeth."

"Never mind my white teeth! Do you know where she keeps her eggs?"

"In the melon bed, on the end nearest the wall, where the sun strikes nearly all day. Rikki-tikki, you're not going to eat her eggs?"

"Not eat exactly, no. Darzee, can you fly off to the stables and pretend your wing is broken, and let Nagaina chase you back to this bush? I must get to the melon bed, and if I went there now, she'd see me."

Darzee knew that Nagaina's children were born in eggs like his own, so he didn't think it was fair to kill them. But his wife was a sensible bird, and she knew that a cobra's eggs meant young cobras later on. So she flew from the nest and left Darzee to keep the babies warm. She flew in front of Nagaina and cried out, "My wing is broken! The boy in the house threw a stone at me and broke it."

Nagaina lifted up her head and hissed, "You've picked a bad place to be lame in." And she moved toward the bird, slipping along over the dust.

"The boy broke it with a stone!" cried Darzee's wife.

"Well! It may please you to know that when you're dead, I will deal with him. Before night, the boy in the house will lie very still. Now what's the use of running away? I'm sure to catch you."

But Darzee's wife fluttered on, never leaving the ground, and Nagaina slithered faster.

Rikki-tikki heard them going up the path, and he raced for the end of the melon patch near the wall. There, very cleverly hidden, he found twenty-five small eggs.

"I was just in time," he thought, for he could see the baby cobras curled up inside the skin, and he knew that the minute they were hatched, they could each kill a man or a mongoose. He bit off the tops of the eggs as fast as he could, crushing the deadly young snakes. At last there were only three eggs left. Then he heard Darzee's wife screaming.

"Rikki-tikki! I led Nagaina toward the house, and she has gone onto the porch and—oh, come quickly!—she means killing!"

Rikki-tikki smashed two eggs and, with the third egg in his mouth, scuttled to the porch as fast as he could. Teddy and his mother and father were there at breakfast, but they were not eating anything. They were stone still, and their faces were pale. Nagaina was coiled up within easy striking distance of Teddy's bare leg, and she was swaying back and forth, singing a song of triumph.

"Son of the man who killed Nag," she hissed, "stay still. Keep very still, all three of you. If you move, I strike, and if you do not move, I strike. Oh, foolish people who killed my Nag!"

Teddy's eyes were fixed on his father, but all his father could do was whisper, "Sit still, Teddy. Don't move. Keep still."

Then Rikki-tikki came up and cried, "Turn around, Nagaina! Turn and fight!"

"All in good time," said she, without moving her eyes. "I'll deal with *you* later. Look at your friends, Rikki-tikki. They dare not move, and if you come a step nearer, I strike."

"Look at your eggs in the melon patch," said Rikki-tikki. "Go and look, Nagaina." The snake turned half around and saw the egg. "Give it to me!" she said.

Rikki-tikki held the egg. "What price for a snake's egg? For a young cobra? For the last—the very last—of the brood? The ants are eating all the others, down by the melon patch."

Nagaina spun around, forgetting everything for the sake of the one egg, and Rikki-tikki saw Teddy's father grab Teddy by the shoulder and drag him across the table with the teacups, out of reach of Nagaina.

"Tricked! Tricked! Tricked! *Rikk-tck-tck*!" called Rikki-tikki. "The boy is safe, and it was I—I—I that caught Nag last night in the bathroom. He threw me back and forth, but he could not shake me off. He was dead before the man killed him. I did it. *Rikki-tikki-tck-tck!* Come, Nagaina. Come and fight me."

Nagaina saw she had lost her chance of killing Teddy, and the egg lay between Rikki-tikki's paws. "Give me the egg, Rikki-tikki, and I will go away and never come back," she said.

"Yes, you'll never come back, because you'll be dead. Fight, snake! The man has gone for his gun. Fight!"

Rikki-tikki was bounding all around Nagaina, keeping just out of her reach. Nagaina gathered herself together and struck out at him. Rikki-tikki jumped up and back. Again and again and again she struck, and each time her head hit with a whack on the matting of the porch. Then Rikki-tikki danced in a circle to get behind her, and Nagaina spun around to face him.

Rikki-tikki had forgotten the egg. It lay on the porch. Nagaina came nearer and nearer to it, till at last, while Rikki-tikki was taking a breath, she caught it in her mouth, turned to the steps, and flew down the path, with Rikki-tikki behind her.

Rikki-tikki knew he must catch her or all the trouble would begin again. She headed straight for the long grass by the thornbush, and as he was running, Rikki-tikki heard Darzee still singing his song of triumph. But Darzee's wife was smarter. She flew off her nest as Nagaina came along and flapped her wings at Nagaina's head. Nagaina only lowered her head and went on. But the instant's delay let Rikki-tikki catch up to her, and as she plunged into the hole where she and Nag used to live, his little white teeth were clenched on her tail.

Rikki-tikki went down with her, and very few mongooses—however wise and old they may be—care to follow a cobra into its hole. It was dark in the hole, and Rikki-tikki never knew when it might widen and give Nagaina room to turn and strike at him.

When the grass by the mouth of the hole stopped waving, Darzee said, "It is all over with Rikki-tikki! We must sing his death song, for Nagaina will surely kill him underground." So he sang a very mournful song that he had just made up, and right at the saddest part, the grass quivered again, and Rikki-tikki dragged himself out of the hole, leg by leg, licking his whiskers. Rikki-tikki shook some of the dust out of his fur and sneezed. "It's all over," he said. "The snake will never come out again." And the red ants that live between the grass stems heard him and began to troop down the hole to see if he had spoken the truth.

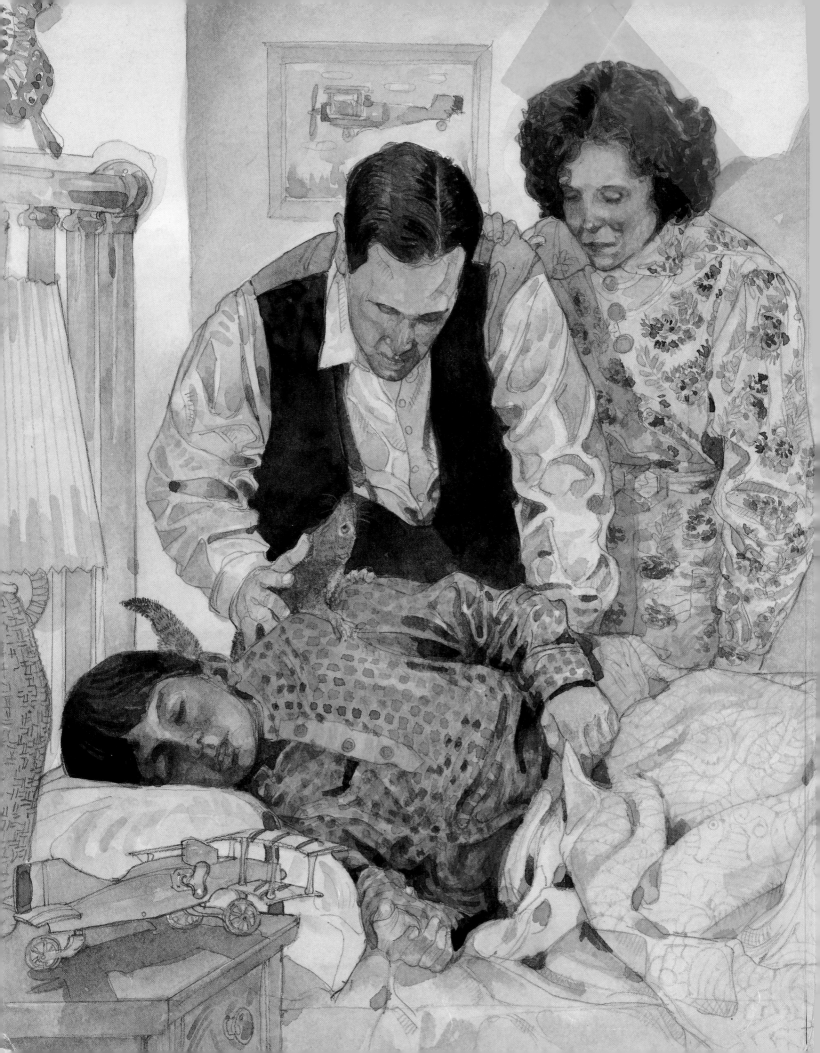

When Rikki got to the house, Teddy and Teddy's mother and Teddy's father came out and almost cried over him. And that night he ate everything that was given to him until he could eat no more. He went to bed on Teddy's shoulder, where Teddy's mother saw him when she looked in late at night.

"He saved our lives," she said to her husband. "Just think, he saved all our lives."

Rikki-tikki woke with a jump, for all mongooses are light sleepers. "Oh, it's you," said he. "What are you awake for? All the cobras are dead, and if they weren't, I'm here."

Rikki-tikki had a right to be proud of himself. And he kept the garden as a mongoose should keep it, with tooth and jump and spring and bite, till never a cobra dared show its head inside the walls.

AFTERWORD

After creating pictures for more than seventy-five books for children, I illustrated the first one where the story occupied a warm place in my own growing-up years. That book was *The Tales of Uncle Remus,* a collection of Brer Rabbit stories retold by Julius Lester. The experience of rediscovering my love for Brer Rabbit tales made me think about the possibility of retrieving other stories I grew up loving.

One that stood out in memory was *The Jungle Book,* with its fantastic world of talking animals who live in an exotic land. As a young person I wished to explore faraway lands and listen in as animals conversed with one another, so I was deeply inspired by the imaginary world Rudyard Kipling conjured. The stories left an indelible impression on me.

I was given the opportunity to express those long-cherished memories through paintings when I illustrated a Books of Wonder edition of *The Jungle Book.* We followed Kipling's preferred selection of Mowgli stories, starting from the baby's being taken in by wolves and continuing through his many adventures learning the ways of the jungle. And we added one more tale: that of Rikki-tikki-tavi. Rikki made his spirited presence known, and we just had to include him.

But *The Jungle Book* contains many wonderful tales to illustrate, and there wasn't room for all that I wanted to show of Rikki's story. Rikki needed to explore the garden of rosebushes and orange trees, to evade the deadly little snakeling and leap out of harm's way from Nag, to visit with his newfound friends Darzee the tailorbird and Darzee's wife, and to jump on Teddy's shoulder and sleep in his bed. It would take the picture book you hold in your hands to give the frisky and curious Rikki enough room to show himself as the true hero he is.

—*Jerry Pinkney*